THE THIEF

THE THIEF

by Thomas Rockwell

Illustrated by Gail Rockwell

A YEARLING BOOK

Published by
Dell Publishing Co., Inc.
1 Dag Hammarskjold Plaza
New York, New York 10017

For information address Delacorte Press, New York, New York.

Yearling ® TM 913705, Dell Publishing Co., Inc.

ISBN: 0-440-48739-0

Reprinted by arrangement with Delacorte Press

Printed in the United States of America
Third Dell printing—November 1981

CW

THE THIEF

I

Tim turned and started toward the stairs.
Larry grabbed him.

"Come on. What have you got?"

"It's *mine*. It was all my own money."

Larry wrestled him down and sat on him,
holding his wrists. Peter wrenched at his
fingers.

"It's mine! You wouldn't give me any of
yours yesterday!"

"Mrs. Turner'll hear him," whispered Peter.

Larry hitched up so that his leg was across
Tim's mouth. Tim squirmed, kicking, gasping,

Larry's corduroy pants pressing against his mouth, and managed to twist his head to the side so he could breathe—he lay still.

"Okay. I got it." Peter stood up.

Larry slid his leg off Tim's head, still holding his wrists down. Tim glanced up at him, squirmed. A glob of spit dangled from Larry's lips, lower and lower. Tim tried to wriggle free, his face turned away.

Peter stuck a piece of gum in his mouth. "Come on. I got the gum."

Larry hitched up so that Tim's head was between his knees. Leaning over him, grinning, he hawked and sucked as if he were gathering a huge glob of spit. Tim tried to hump his body, wrench himself free. He couldn't even turn his head now. Larry's knees were hurting his arms. He gave up, tears starting in his eyes, helpless, maybe Larry'd just . . . Larry let go of his wrists and got roughly off him.

"You would have been so smeared . . ."

Ducking under the slanting roof, Larry and Peter went off to their room. Tim sat up, wiping his eyes on his sleeve. He picked up the packet of gum. They'd taken four sticks and left him only one. Mrs. Turner would just tell him to stay away from them; he'd thought they were still in the living room watching television. Larry had seen him put his hand in his pocket to hide the gum.

He went downstairs and through the kitchen. Mrs. Turner was reading her newspaper in the rocking chair by the stove. She glanced over it at him, turning a page.

"What're you boys doing up there? You ain't into anything?"

"No."

Tim ran his hand over the polished surface of the dining-room table. In the front hall he stopped to look out the narrow window beside the door. The leaves were almost all gone from the trees. It had stopped raining. A gust of wind spattered drops from the trees across the puddles in the leaf-strewn road. Someone was coming across the bridge . . . a boy. He came on up the road past the church standing all by itself on the green, the fields yellow and wet behind it. Across the road there was a car parked in front of the Grange Hall. A few weeks ago a new family had moved into the run-down house across the river beside old Mrs. Mears' and the Woodwards'—a rusty car up on blocks in the front yard, piles of old lumber; cardboard in one of the upstairs windows. A family with a baby had lived there before . . . the baby playing on the porch with an old spoon and some pans.

"TA-TAHHH!"

Behind him the door of the stairs banged open. Tim ducked, squirmed into the dining room, one shoe coming off. They had the toy handcuffs, ropes. He scrambled up the back stairs. Larry grabbed for him at the top, pulling off his other shoe. A chair clattered over. Tim tripped on the rug in the hall, trampled down the front stairs—Mrs. Turner yelling from the kitchen—worked frantically at the front door bolt, snatched open the door, and ran out onto the front lawn. . . . He stopped, his stockinged feet sinking into the soggy lawn. . . . The front door slammed behind him, the bolt clicked. He glimpsed Mrs. Turner going back through the dining room. She'd probably made Larry and Peter go back upstairs. He lifted his foot to look at his muddy sock. The boy was watching him from the road.

"My shoes came off." Tim shrugged.

"They wouldn't mess with me like that,"

said the boy. "I'd get 'em some way. How old are they?"

"Thirteen and twelve."

"Crud. . . . You ever seen anybody hit with brass knuckles?"

Tim shook his head.

"I seen a man up in Pownal once, busted his jaw right off almost."

"What had he done?"

"I don't know, messin' around with somebody probably. Your father has that racing car, doesn't he?"

"Yeah."

"My brother used to drive stock cars. Crud. He didn't care who he hit. He'd smash anybody."

Tim glanced down at his feet, wiggling his toes. Maybe he should take off his socks and just run around to the back door barefoot.

"Where's your father keep his car?"

"In the garage. It doesn't have any motor."

"How come?"

"He sold it last year. He's been trying to sell the car, too. You want to see it?"

They went around the house. "I gotta get my shoes and the key," Tim said.

One of the cats waiting on the back porch squirmed through his legs as he tried to shut the door. He caught it by the tail and dumped it back out. Mrs. Turner had put his shoes on the stairs. He found a dry pair of socks in the laundry room and went back out onto the porch and sat down on the steps.

"How come you got so many cats?" asked the boy.

Two of the kittens had begun to play with the laces of the shoes.

"I don't know." Tim pulled off his wet socks. At breakfast that morning Larry had started in on him about the cats again. Dad had said something about why couldn't he find homes for just a few of them anyway. Just the ones he can't tell the names of, Larry'd said, that'd be fair. Peter had chimed in. Finally Mom had made them stop: everyone had agreed months ago that as long as Tim kept the cats outside and took care of them himself, he could keep up to eight . . .

Tim heaved up the garage door. The midget racer was on a trailer.

"You ever drive it?" asked the boy.

"No."

Larry and Peter had always helped Dad

work on the car. Even if Tim had been closest to a tool, they'd pushed him away or made him hand it to them first. It hadn't been any fun standing around getting shoved out of the way all the time. If he yelled or anything, Dad just sent them all back to the house.

"How fast did it go?"

"I don't know. I guess about eighty or ninety. Don't climb on it. My father doesn't let anyone in it unless he's here."

"Crud. If you pulled the door down, no one'd see us."

"My brothers would tell."

"Yeah. Crud. My sister's always blabbin' on me. Then she runs and hides behind someone so I can't get her."

"You want to see his old crash helmet? It's in the house."

Up in the playroom, the boy fitted the white crash helmet gingerly over his head. It hid his lank tousled dark hair so that he looked younger, almost baby-faced. Tim showed him how to fasten the chin strap. It was too big; the chin cup kept slipping down onto his neck. He looked around the playroom.

"This all your stuff?"

"Some of it."

Tim kept most of his toys in his room. Otherwise Larry and Peter always tried to say everything was theirs. The electric train was part his. Tim showed the boy how to run it, kneeling by the transformer. The boy didn't act as know-it-all as he had out in the garage. Tim had to show him how to couple and uncouple the cars. The telephone rang downstairs in the kitchen. They heard Mrs. Turner answer it.

"Is she your grandmother?" the boy asked.

"No. She just comes and cooks dinner four days a week so my mother'll have time to do other stuff."

"Oh." The boy fitted the caboose onto the track.

"You want to see what's fun?" said Tim. "If we jack the track up on blocks and then race the engine off it, like it was going over a cliff? I'll get some pillows."

He went off to his room. Larry and Peter were always doing stuff like this. He stacked the pillows at the end of the track.

"It sort of scares you. You know, if it misses the pillows?"

"You wouldn't have *nothin'* left. Crud. I bet it'd bust the floor. You got everything off that side?"

"Wait."

Tim was gathering up the disconnected switches and crossing gates and streetlights and piling them up beside the bookcase. The boy just left everything scattered around; something might get kneeled on and broken.

Somebody was coming up the stairs. Tim stood up. If it was Larry or Peter . . .

A little girl. The boy turned back to the switch he was prying up. "What you want?"

The little girl looked around the playroom. "The lady said you was up here."

"What you want?"

"Ma's lookin' for you."

"Tell her I'm busy."

"Dwayne, you better come. She says you didn't get in the wood this morning, and she's gonna tell Daddy when he comes home if you don't."

"How'd she know where I was? You tell her?"

"Buddy did. . . . I seen that on TV." She pointed at the Chitty-Chitty-Bang-Bang car on the bookshelf.

"Crud." Dwayne stood up and started to take off the crash helmet. "Go on. I'm comin'." He glanced at Tim. "I gotta go."

Tim heard the back door slam. He went into Larry and Peter's room and watched Dwayne and his sister going down the road toward the bridge. They didn't pay any attention to each other, Dwayne getting farther and farther ahead. He'd seen Dwayne's mother on their porch last week, a pale, thin woman wearing a man's torn leather jacket over her dress. . . .

After lunch, when Larry and Peter found the mess in the playroom—tracks and pillows scattered about, all the switches and lights in a pile by the bookcase—they made Tim stop watching television and come upstairs to put everything back the way it had been. He crawled around gathering stuff together. Larry and Peter began to make train wrecks, wedging a block or wad of paper in the tracks. After a while they decided to change everything—to a city, factories, a river. Larry crawled into the long closet under the slanting roof to get the cardboard factories and buildings; Peter began to pull all the tracks apart. Tim wandered off to his room and dragged his box of comic books out from under his bed. After a while Mrs. Turner called up the stairs to him; Dwayne appeared in the door.

"What're you doin'?" He looked around the room. "You want to run the trains again?"

"My brothers are playing with them."

Dwayne sat down on the bed. "I got about *five thousand* comics," he said.

"You want to play soldiers?"

Sometimes Tim spent all afternoon setting up his soldiers and tanks and artillery in two armies, one by his bed, the other under his table. Then he'd fight a battle, lying on the floor, the bed and table towering above him like mesas, soldiers and tanks charging up out of the ditch far away across the fuzzy desert of the rug. At night he shut the doors of his room and turned off the lights so he could use the kitchen flashlight as a searchlight — patrols trapped in no-man's-land, sirens, planes taking off into the darkness from the airfield on the bed . . .

"Okay." Dwayne shrugged.

He started to line up his tanks and cannons and trucks in two long rows on the edge of the rug. Tim watched him. He didn't know how to play soldiers, either.

"You can make machine-gun nests out of the blocks." He showed Dwayne how to build a fort in the legs of the chair, set up observation posts on the table. The back door slammed. They heard Larry and Peter's voices outside.

Dwayne got up. "I guess I'll go look at the trains."

Tim rearranged the rest of Dwayne's army, set up a hospital and supply depot for him in the corner under the table. When he finally went down the hall to the playroom, Dwayne was trying Larry's Swiss army knife on the rafters in the closet. He'd started to build the ramp for the tracks again.

"Crud. This ain't even sharp."

"You want to finish with the soldiers?"

"Naw. Come on." Dwayne crawled out of the closet. "Let's do the trains."

After that, Dwayne came almost every day. He never asked Tim if it'd be all right or anything; he just showed up. They hardly ever saw each other at school because Tim was in one of the special open classes.

Sometimes Tim wished he wouldn't come as much. If Dwayne wanted to do something, he just went ahead and did it no matter what

Tim said—like pushing trucks off the side of the bed to see them crack up. If he was looking for something, he'd dump the whole box of toys out on the floor. . . . At least Tim didn't have to wander around after Larry and Peter anymore or sit on his bed listening to them playing in their room . . . Mom's typewriter clicking downstairs . . . if he went in, they'd just yell at him. Dwayne boasted a lot about all the stuff he had at home, but he never asked Tim over. Tim saw him once walking on the road near Bentley's Store with a tall red-haired man.

"There's Dwayne," he said to his mother.

She didn't stop to give them a ride. Tim glanced back as the car passed them. Neither Dwayne nor his father looked up.

Dwayne always acted as if he didn't notice Larry or Peter—even if they started teasing Tim or trying to make him do something. Now and then he'd glance at them. When they were out somewhere, he'd go into their room and look at stuff and fool around.

II

Tim was eating his cereal, reading a comic book propped up against the orange juice pitcher. Larry was complaining to their mother about something.

"I bet *I* know who's doing it," said Peter.

Tim glanced up. His mother and Larry and Peter were all looking at him.

"What?"

"Now, Peter," said their mother.

"I don't mean Tim," said Peter. "I mean that poor kid, Dwayne what's-his-name."

"Hey, yeah." Larry stopped lacing his boot.

"That's when the stuff started disappearing. Remember? Because it was the day Mrs. Turner said Peter and me couldn't go up in the woods, the day you weren't here, and then you came back and said we could and then I couldn't find my knife."

"I caught him once looking in my drawers," said Peter. "I came in and he was standing right by my bureau, the drawers all hanging open? So I asked him what he was doing, but he just mumbled something and went back to Tim's room."

"The .22 bullets, my compass, my Corgi Ferrari, Peter's ammunition pouch."

"Yeah, but you're always losing things," said Tim. "Last winter you lost your knife and then two months later Mrs. Turner found it behind the radiator."

"Yeah? How could I lose a whole box of .22 shells, sitting right on top of the books? And my compass was in my *drawer*."

"It didn't even *work*. It's never worked since you got it."

"Yeah, but he didn't know it."

"Tim. That's enough, Larry." Their mother turned to the stove with her coffee cup. Tim straightened up his comic book. How could Dwayne have been stealing stuff? He'd have acted nervous or something, said he had to go home early a lot. Tim would have noticed something. That time in Cape Cod when Tim had wanted to borrow the TV Magic cards from that boy without telling him. . . . He'd been so afraid the boy would find out or something. . . . Finally he'd just put the cards back in the drawer. He hadn't been able to find the Solido howitzer last night, but it was probably way back under the bed or somewhere.

His mother set the coffeepot back on the stove. "Tim, the things that are missing may be just lost, like Larry's knife last winter . . ."

"Yeah, but Mrs. Turner found that, but she hasn't found any of this stuff," Larry said.

"Larry, wait. But Tim, Dwayne's family doesn't have everything we have, and he may not be able to resist the temptation to take something home just . . ."

"He doesn't. I'd have seen him."

"How about the times you're in your room and he's in the playroom? Like yesterday when . . ."

"I still saw him before he went home. He . . ."

"*Larry. Tim.* Wait till I've finished. If Dwayne is taking things home without asking, we should try to help him. He seems like a nice boy. He hasn't taken anything valuable . . ."

"My Swiss army knife?"

"Larry, wait. And he probably won't. But think how you would feel if your family didn't have everything and you saw what you three boys have—trains and chemistry sets and games. After he gets used to it, he probably won't want to take things home without asking. He'll know we won't mind if he asks to borrow something. But for a while maybe we should all try as much as possible to put things away, just until he gets used to us. Don't leave things like your knives or your allowances lying out, and then he won't be tempted."

"Yeah, but what about *my* knife?"

"Larry, we don't know that he took it."

"You can't prove it," said Peter. "If you asked him, he'd just say he didn't. And you haven't got any clues, like if a button had fallen off his shirt into your drawer."

"We know he was here."

Tim wondered what the inside of Dwayne's

19

house was like. He'd been in Jimmy Skidmore's kitchen once. Jimmy had had to get his boots so they could go sliding behind Squire's; Tim had waited just inside the door. Jimmy's mother hadn't even looked at him, shuffling about the littered kitchen, so fat he could hear her breathing over the noise of the television set from the next room—the lunch dishes still on the table, dirty dishes and tin cans piled in the sink, heaps of clothes all over, cupboard doors hanging open. He'd stood there scraping the edge of his boot along a tear in the lino-leum. If he'd looked up, Jimmy's mother might have thought he was noticing how messy and dirty everything was. The kitchen had smelled like babies' diapers—maybe it had been the piles of old clothes . . . Dwayne's mother wasn't fat. His Levi's were worn and grimy, the cuffs of his jacket frayed.

"Why can't we just tell him he can't come in anymore?" said Larry. "Tim and him can play outside. We can't hide *everything*."

"You probably *hid* the knife," said Tim. "So they'd buy you a new one. You wrecked the corkscrew and the punch trying to open the glue that time."

"So what? I still wouldn't try to hide it to get a new one."

"He wouldn't have looked all over for it if he'd hid it," said Peter. "He'd have just pretended."

Someone knocked on the back door. Their mother hung up the dish towel and went into the entryway.

"Oh. Dwayne. How are you?"

Tim couldn't hear Dwayne's reply.

"Come in. We've finished breakfast. Tim. Dwayne's here."

Tim had expected him to look different somehow—tougher, squinting a little as if he was hiding something—but he looked the same, his round pale sharp-featured face, tousled dark hair. Going up the stairs behind him, Tim wondered if people who stole things thought about stealing all the time. He could see the white skin of his thigh through a hole in his Levi's. They decided to play Monopoly. Peter came and stood in the door, watching Tim explaining the rules. Dwayne always bragged about all the stuff he had, so maybe he hadn't stolen anything; the things had just gotten lost. Peter wandered away. Tim and

Dwayne began a game. The back door slammed, Larry yelled at the cats. Dwayne didn't buy Baltic Avenue. Then he landed on St. James Place and didn't buy that either. Tim wondered if he should explain again. . . . But they were playing a real game, he'd explained everything once. He landed on Luxury Tax and started to count his money.

"I gotta go to the bathroom." Dwayne stood up.

"Yeah, okay." Tim kept on counting. After a minute he stopped and listened. The other door to the bathroom led into his mother and father's room. He put his Luxury Tax in the bank and went out into the hall. The bathroom door was shut; he couldn't hear anything inside. He went on down the hall and looked into his parents' bedroom. Dwayne was standing by the bureau, looking at the photographs of Tim's relatives.

"What're you doing?"

"Nothin'." Dwayne looked around. He didn't act nervous or anything. They went back to Tim's room. After a while Tim's mother called up the stairs. "Tim, I'm going to the market. I'll be back by eleven."

"I gotta go," said Dwayne.

"Why?" Tim had just bought three houses.

"I gotta check my father's traps. He had to go to Pownal."

"What kind of traps? Can I come?"

"Yeah, okay."

III

Dwayne put down the burlap bag and length of pipe and, pushing under some bushes, hauled a trap out of the water. Squatting, he scraped the mud off it with a stick and then yanked the chain to make sure it was still fastened.

"Did a muskrat take the bait?" asked Tim.

"You don't use any. This is one of their runs."

Dwayne laid the trap on a firm, grassy place on the bank and set his feet carefully on the springs, forcing the jaws of the trap open.

Reaching down, he wedged the trigger against the base of the plate, cocking the trap, and then stepped off it.

"Aren't you scared you'll get your fingers caught?"

"Crud." Dwayne set the trap in the water and shoved it under the bushes with the stick. "There." He wiped his mouth. "I saw a kid once who'd stepped in one. They had to *cut* his boot off, his toes all mashed."

As Dwayne hauled the next trap up out of the shadowy water, a dead muskrat emerged, rolling over onto its back, its fur waterlogged, its orange teeth gleaming in its grizzled snout. Dwayne poked it with the pipe, then opened the trap.

"Did it kill it just having its leg caught?"

"Naw, it drowned. That's why the trap's hooked to something." Dwayne cocked the trap and stepped off it. "When it tries to swim away, it drowns."

The next trap was empty, still cocked under the clear, quiet water.

"It's almost like some weird animal, waiting for something to poke it to see what it is." Tim had sort of an eerie feeling—the trap

looked so harmless and quiet under the water.

Dwayne shrugged, ducking under a bush which overhung the path.

"See him? Crud."

The chain disappeared under the log. Back in the dimness Tim saw something move . . . as if it was trying to push further back.

"How are you going to get him out?"

"We gotta get poles. Crud. He's liable to run right up along the chain if we try to pull him out." Dwayne glanced at the length of pipe. "Pa's so quick. He just snakes them out and hits them."

Tim's pole kept catching in the punky wood; the muskrat scrambled back and forth under the log, hissing, the chain rattling. Tim's arms ached; he was sweating. He stopped poking and scrounging with the pole. Once or twice he'd felt something soft, the muskrat's stomach or neck? The knees of his pants were wet from kneeling in the leaves.

"This ain't gonna work." Dwayne put down his pole.

"Maybe if we just poke him real hard."

Dwayne's face was red. He was sweating, too.

"Naw. If we hurt his fur, he's no good." Dwayne bent down to peer at the muskrat huddled in the dimness under the log.

"Suppose you just come back in a few days? Wouldn't he starve to death?"

"Something else would get him, dogs or something. You think you can pull him out by yourself far enough so I can hit him?"

"You said he'd run up along the chain."

"Naw. All you'd have to do is drop it."

Tim dragged a fallen sapling aside so he'd have a clear path behind him through the underbrush. He wasn't sure how fast a muskrat could run. If the chain broke, the muskrat would go for the water, wouldn't it?

"Come on. What're you doing?" said Dwayne.

"Okay." Tim picked up the chain. "I'll call go. One, two, three . . ." Dwayne was peering over the log from the back, holding the pipe. ". . . GO!"

Tim yanked on the chain, pulled, dragging the muskrat slowly out . . . as if it was digging in its claws . . . the chain jerked loose, Tim fell over backwards . . . rolling, scrambling on hands and knees into the bushes, the muskrat after him?

"Crud!" Thunk.

The muskrat writhing and rolling beside the log, Dwayne hitting at it with the pipe. "Come *on*! Hit it! I can't reach him!"

Tim grabbed one of the poles.

"In the neck, break his neck!"

Tim kept missing, hitting the pipe, the log. It was like trying to hit a fish flopping on the bank. He didn't dare get too close, the rattling chain . . . He realized suddenly the muskrat wasn't moving anymore; it was them—hitting it, banging it about. He backed away, dragging the pole. Dwayne was panting. The muskrat lay still on its back.

"Crud."

One of the muskrat's claws jerked convulsively; its lips looked as if they were grinning bloodily.

Dwayne poked it with the pipe. "He's deader'n a stone."

Tim remembered a poem his mother had read him and Larry and Peter once—about a badger captured in the woods and then let loose in the town and chased with dogs and sticks till everybody thought it was dead; then it would suddenly start up again, driving everybody back. . . .

Dwayne picked up a pole and prodded the muskrat over onto its stomach.

"Crud. His fur looks all right."

They gazed at the dead muskrat. Tim felt his sweaty clothes getting cold. Ratty in *The Wind in the Willows* had been a muskrat. . . . He hadn't realized what they were doing . . . killing something, beating it to death. . . .

"You comin'?"

Tim put down the pole, then picked it up. "Aren't you going to put him in the bag with the others?"

"We'll get him when we come back."

The ice in the shallow puddles crackled under their feet. They found two more dead muskrats. In another trap there was just the claw of a muskrat.

"Crud, he chewed his own leg off." Dwayne scraped the mud off the trap with a stick.

Tim touched the claw with his shoe. "My father told me once about a man who cut off three of his own toes because they'd frozen. Otherwise he would have gotten gangrene and died. Are you going to keep it?"

"Naw. What good is it?"

"Yeah." Tim put the claw in his pocket.

*　*　*

When they got back to Dwayne's house, his father's rusty pickup truck was parked in front. Tim followed Dwayne around to the back. His father came out of one of the sheds.

"How many you get?" He took the burlap bag from Dwayne.

"Four. One chewed itself out."

His father emptied the bag on a shelf along the outside of the shed and, rummaging a knife out of the litter of tools and bits and pieces of machinery, began to skin one of the muskrats. His face looked too old to have so many freckles—the little wrinkles around his eyes and thin mouth. He scraped the guts of the muskrat into a pail under the shelf.

"Goddamn it, what'd you do to this one?"

"He got in under a log."

"Crud." He cut down the muskrat's belly from the tip of the chin to the tail, flicking back the skin with the point of the knife. Then he cut off the claws and the head—as if he was cutting nothing, cabbage, a potato—and worked the hide off, pulling on it and at the same time slicing deftly under it where it clung to the carcass. He laid the skinned carcasses on the burlap bag, tossing the skins together on the litter at the back of the shelf. The carcasses were so white, the flesh pink under the white membrane and fat.

"Take 'em in to your Ma."

He went into the shed. Dwayne gathered up the burlap bag with the carcasses on it.

"I guess I gotta go," said Tim.

"Yeah." Dwayne went toward the house, the bag knocking against his legs.

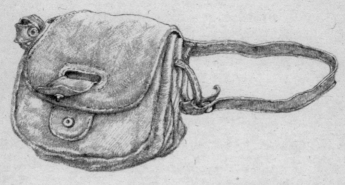

IV

"He really charged right at you?" Peter took another cookie from the plate.

"Yeah. And then I didn't think we'd ever be able to finish him off. He was rolling and writhing around, all tangled up in the chain; we kept hitting each other's pole instead of him. Dwayne's father yelled at him because we'd banged his fur all up. Mr. Bentley pays them twelve dollars each."

"Yeah, but the traps probably cost a lot," said Larry.

"They made forty-eight dollars." Peter had

worked it out on the edge of his comic book. "You can use the traps over and over."

Their mother came in from the other room with her coffee cup.

"Can people eat muskrats?" Larry asked.

She set the cup in the sink. "Yes. Tim, would you come to my study for a minute."

"See?" said Peter to Larry. "I told you."

"Yeah, but that doesn't mean that they do."

Tim followed his mother through the dining room. He couldn't remember anything he'd done.

"Sit." His mother smiled at him and patted her desk chair. She sat down in the chair by the window. "Did you find your sandwich in the refrigerator?"

"Yeah."

"Tim, something else has happened. This morning Daddy gave me twenty-five dollars for the shopping, but when I opened my bag at the market, there was only ten dollars."

Tim reached out and shut the top of the little stamp box on the desk.

"Were you with Dwayne all the time he was here this morning?"

"Yes."

"You didn't leave him even for a few minutes, to go to the bathroom or into the play-room?"

"I don't know." It was like she was blaming him.

"Where did you go when you went out?"

"Down by the river, to see if there was anything in his father's traps."

"Tim, look at me. Are you sure he's the kind of boy you want to be friends with? If we can't trust him, if we have to watch him every minute he's here?"

Tim kept opening and shutting the stamp box. Every time he shut it, the lid caught a little, so that he had to push it down tight. Dwayne had had the money in his pocket the whole time? When they were kneeling to-gether in the leaves trying to poke the muskrat out from under the log . . . watching his father skin the muskrats?

"Tim?"

"What?"

"If you really like him, I don't want to say he can't come here. I know there aren't any other boys your age near us now that Jimmy has moved away. But it's so difficult to have someone coming in and out of the house that we can't trust."

Tim almost said an old broken knife and a few .22 shells didn't make any difference. But then he remembered the money. He shrugged. It could have been someone else—Mrs. Turner, Larry or Peter. Mrs. Turner hadn't come yet. . . . "Maybe Daddy just took it back without telling you because he had to pay someone."

"No."

Tim picked at the edge of the stamp box with his fingernail.

"Well, if you really think you want to keep him as a friend . . . But you'll have to promise me to stay with him whenever he comes in, not to leave him for a moment."

He didn't dare say Larry or Peter might have taken it just to get him. Now that Dwayne was around, they couldn't gang up on him all the time. He hated them. He didn't care if they died or went blind and . . .

"Will you promise? And I think you should just play with him in your room or the playroom. Don't let him roam through the whole house or into Peter's and Larry's room."

He picked at the edge of the stamp box. He didn't care. It'd been fun about some things, like the muskrats, but Dwayne always wanted

to do just what *he* wanted. He hadn't remembered about his father's traps until Tim had started winning at Monopoly.

"Tim?"

"Yeah, okay."

He went up to his room. The money could have fallen out of her pocketbook while she was at the market. He tried to imagine Dwayne sliding his hand into the half-open drawer, glancing around to make sure nobody was coming. . . . It could have been a pickpocket. In Ancram, in the A & P? He could have been on his way to Albany and just stopped off at the A & P to buy a soda or something. Tim began to put the Monopoly set back in its box.

"Boy, fifteen dollars." Larry and Peter came into the room.

"He could get put in jail for that if Mom wanted to call the police."

Larry sat down on the bed. "You know when he did it?"

Tim didn't answer.

"He probably said he was going to the bathroom and then just went through the other door and took it out of Mom's pocketbook and came back through the bathroom," said Peter. "Is she gonna let him come in anymore?"

Tim put the rubber band around the deeds. "He didn't go to the bathroom."

"If I catch him in our room, I'll search him," said Larry, "make him pull out all his pockets, even take off his sneakers."

"He could swallow it," said Peter.

"And if he *still* steals something," Larry said to Tim, "you have to pay because you're letting him come in."

"You can't prove he took anything," said Tim. "You're always losing stuff. The money could have just dropped out of Mom's pocketbook."

"Then why'd it never happen before? He comes around and all of a sudden everybody starts losing stuff?"

"You lost your knife before."

"Yeah, and then I found it, but I haven't . . ."

"You didn't find it, Mrs. Turner did."

"What about the other things?" said Peter. "The .22 bullets, the . . ."

"Come on." Larry got up. "Don't argue with him. He's just a little sissy anyway. He never admits he's wrong."

They went off into the playroom. Tim put

the Monopoly box away under his bed and then began to set up his soldiers. Larry and Peter always blamed everything on him. . . . They probably didn't even know what a muskrat trap looked like. . . . Tim took his bank out of the drawer of his bed table and counted his money. Next Friday when he got his allowance, he'd have enough for the Russian machine-gun squad at Haber's. He wondered what muskrat tasted like. He could have asked Dwayne to save him a piece . . .

V

"If he doesn't come today, it proves it, because he was here almost every day before," said Peter. "He never stayed away five days."

"He might have to help his father again," said Tim, finishing his cereal.

"Yeah, but there's no school today or tomorrow so he'd have *some* time off. His father wouldn't make him work the whole vacation."

"You're lying," Larry said to Tim. "How come he never had to help his father before?"

"Larry, stop it," said their mother. "Let Tim alone."

She went into the laundry room with the basket of clothes.

Larry whispered to Tim. "He knows if he comes back, Mom won't let him in so he won't get a chance to steal anything, so what's the use of coming."

"Or he's out shooting up all our .22 bullets," said Peter.

Tim put his dish in the sink and went outside, pushing the cats out of the way. Behind the garage he picked up the basketball. Even if he was still too short to dribble between his legs, he should be able to dribble behind his back. But he could never get turned around fast enough, the ball always bounced away. He heard his father's car start, the tires crunching on the gravel. If he bounced the ball first with his left hand . . . the kitchen door slammed. The click of the croquet mallets, Larry and Peter talking . . . they'd just knock his ball into the bushes; Mom wouldn't want to play now. He put the basketball down and peered around the side of the garage until Larry and Peter were both turned the other way, arguing about something, and then ran quietly across the driveway and down the side of the house. He wandered down to the bridge. The water swept past the abutment, gurgling, splashing, disappearing endlessly into the shadow of the bridge. Sometimes it splashed higher, the drops drying quickly away into the concrete. There wasn't anyone in the backyard of Dwayne's house. Maybe he was sick. Tim wandered down the road. A cat was sleeping on the porch. He went on past. Mr. Woodward was splitting wood in his driveway. Tim decided to go back and try to fix the truck he'd stepped on going to the bathroom in the middle of the night last week. Dwayne's little sister was making a mud pie in the front yard. He stopped to watch her.

"Dwayne's out back," she said, drawing on the pie with a stick.

Tim picked his way slowly along the path through the leaf-strewn junk and old lumber, hoping Dwayne's father and mother weren't around. He found Dwayne behind one of the sheds, rubbing the stock of a gun with an old rag.

"Hi. What're you doing?"

Dwayne looked up. "Nothin'. Oiling my gun."

Tim watched him pour more oil on the rag. The oil darkened the worn, scratched wood of the stock as he rubbed and rubbed. Tim glanced at his face. His lips were chapped; he had a tiny black mole by his nose. What would he do if Tim suddenly told him Larry and Peter, Mom, everybody knew he was stealing stuff from them?

"What kind of a gun is it?"

"Twenty-two."

A screen door slammed at the house next door. Tim heard old Mrs. Mears talking. A dog yipped, chain rattled.

"My father won't let me have a gun till I'm fourteen."

Dwayne grunted.

A car turned into the driveway of the Grange Hall across the river. A woman got out. Dwayne screwed the top onto the jar of oil. His hands were so chapped, the skin on his knuckles had cracked and bled. . . . What if Tim just charged into him all of a sudden, punching and kicking, yelling he was a *thief*?

Dwayne wrapped the gun in an old burlap bag and squeezed into the shed between two loose boards. He came back without the gun and set the jar of oil behind the boards.

"You want to play Monopoly or something?" asked Tim.

"Okay."

They went back through the front yard. Dwayne's sister had left her mud-pie pans scattered about.

Maybe he'd be too scared to take anything else. . . . Tim would have had to spend the whole vacation wandering around by himself; Larry and Peter just kept teasing him.

Dwayne stopped to look at a hawk drifting overhead. Tim wondered if he'd ever stolen anything from a store, if he'd ever broken into someone's house at night. Maybe he didn't care what anybody said. As long as no one caught him or made him give the stuff back . . . Maybe he just never thought about it. . . .

Tim's mother came out of the kitchen drying her hands on a towel when she heard the door.

"Hello, Dwayne." She spoke coldly, looking directly at him. Dwayne mumbled. She acted like that when she wanted someone to know she was angry. "Tim, remember what I asked you, all right?"

"Yeah, okay."

They went up to Tim's room and got out the Monopoly set. Dwayne kept fooling around, zooming the little tin car all around the board, dropping blacks on the Jail with one of Tim's airplanes.

"Come on. Cut it out." Tim straightened his stacks of money. "Put the plane back."

"Boom!" Dwayne dropped a block on the piles of deeds and messed them with his hand.

"Come on. You're messing up everything." Tim grabbed the block.

"Gimme it."

They struggled. Dwayne shoved him against

the bed table. A box of soldiers slid onto the floor, the table crashed over.

For a moment neither of them moved, waiting to see if anyone had heard.

"Tim?" his mother called from downstairs. "Tim, what are you doing?"

"The table fell over." He laid the lamp on the bed. Dwayne was picking up the Chance cards.

"Did you break anything?"

"No, it's okay." Tim tried the lamp.

"If you want to wrestle, Tim, you and Dwayne had better go outside."

"We weren't wrestling." He picked up the box of soldiers.

"Well, please be more careful."

"Yeah, okay."

Tim sat down on the bed. "You want to do something else?"

"I don't know. . . . Hey, you want to see a crazy man?"

"Where?"

"Up that road by the farm with the blue silos."

VI

Kneeling in the bushes behind the stone wall, they watched the half-open back door of the small, weather-beaten house. A chopping block stood in the middle of the patch of trampled dirt by the door, slabwood scattered about. Through a broken window a gray, torn curtain stirred now and then. The roof shingles were greenish with moss. A limb from the huge gray dead elm beside the house had fallen across the chimney, breaking off some of the bricks.

Dwayne stood up and threw another stone at the house. Nothing happened. Somewhere up the wall a chipmunk chirped.

"Crud. I'll wake him up this time if he's sleeping."

A tinkle of breaking glass, the top of the curtain billowed in. They waited, watching the door.

"Come on. He can't be in there. Let's go look inside."

The door squeaked slowly open when Dwayne pushed it. The gray, weathered boards were rotted away on the bottom. Tim couldn't make out much in the dimness—a heap of rags on a chair, the end of a box. He smelled kerosene.

"Anybody here?" called Dwayne.

"Suppose he's around front?" whispered Tim.

"Go look."

Tim went around through the weeds to the front of the house. There was no one. A path led down to the road. He went back around the house.

"Yeah, but suppose he comes while we're inside?"

"We'd hear him. He's always talking to himself coming along the road from the store." Dwayne pushed the door further open and stepped inside. "Come on."

A narrow path through junk—old furniture, boxes, a pail hanging from the ceiling. Light gleamed through the cracks of an inner door onto a worn scrap of rug.

"Crud." A clatter. Dwayne pushed open the inner door.

A small room lit by the afternoon sunlight through grimy windows: a table covered with faded oilcloth . . . a few dishes, a sugar bowl, bottle of ketchup—the sides smeared, turning black. A mound of coats hung on the back of the front door—wallpaper peeling off the walls —tattered, yellowing curtains on the windows.

They edged into the room. There was a small stove beside the side window. Dwayne took a can from a shelf over the stove. A jar tumbled off and broke.

The smell of kerosene almost made Tim sick. How could somebody live in a place like this? The old kerosene heater was dented, smudged with soot. There was another room through a half-open door on the left.

"Come on, let's go. Suppose he comes back?"

"Crud." Dwayne was dumping stuff into a big pot on the stove. "Hold it. I'm making him some soup." He emptied the sugar bowl into the pot, the ketchup, slopped in some water from a pail sitting just inside the pantry beside the stove.

"There." He began to fill the dishes on the table with an old ladle, dripping the glop across the floor, table.

"You're getting it all over."

"So what? I bet he thinks it's the best soup he's ever had." Dwayne took a milk carton from the windowsill and ladled glop into it, then dropped the ladle back into the pot and went into the pantry. Tim could hear him rummaging about. "Crud, I never seen such junk." He came out of the pantry and went into the bedroom.

"I'm going," said Tim.

"Pow!" Dwayne threw a gray, lumpy pillow at him from the door of the bedroom. "Crud." He switched on the light bulb hanging over the table and then swatted it so it swung wildly, almost touching the ceiling.

Tim went back through the dark, cluttered storeroom to the empty yard. It was all right to go in and look, but Dwayne shouldn't wreck stuff. A car passed on the road. Suppose someone found out it'd been them? A path led through the bushes beyond the elm to an old outhouse. He heard Dwayne thumping about in the storeroom.

"Crud." Dwayne came out of the house. "I locked the front door from inside and piled stuff in front of this door. He won't be able to get in."

Dwayne picked up a hatchet and flung it at the elm. It missed, bounding away into the bushes. "Come on. We can hide behind the wall and see what he does."

A truck's brakes squealed in front of the house. Then the engine ground up again, shifting . . . they crouched lower behind the wall. . . .

"He must be trying the front door now."

"Yeah."

The old man shuffled slowly around the corner of the house. His torn overalls hung baggily, greasy with dirt. His beard was a dirty yellowish color around his mouth, his hair matted under his hat.

"What do you think he's saying, mumbling to himself all the time?"

"I don't know. Just crud."

The old man disappeared into the storeroom.

"Wait'll he finds all the stuff piled up."

The old man came out and went slowly back around the corner of the house.

"He can't figure out what's going on. Crud."

The sun was warm in the shelter of the bushes. Tim scratched a scab of lichen off a rock. He hadn't touched anything; Dwayne had done it all. "Let's go."

"Naw, wait. See what he does."

The old man came out of the back door carrying the pot from the stove with both hands.

"Crud. He must've had a key."

The old man dumped out the pot by the chopping block, watching the glop run away among the weeds. Then he shuffled a few steps toward the wall and all of a sudden looked up, right at the bushes where Dwayne and Tim were crouching. The wrinkles of his face were sooty, his eyes red-rimmed.

"Get down," whispered Dwayne.

The old man started toward them, still holding the pot in both hands. "He's seen our tracks in the brush. Go on. Crawl along the wall."

Tim squirmed around.

"Sons a' bitches! I see you. Ever'thing crud. Get my gun."

"*Run.*" Dwayne scrambled past Tim.

Brambles caught at Tim's legs; he stumbled, almost crying, the old man right behind him, about to grab his shoulder; he glanced back: scattered cedars, the stone wall slanting down through the overgrown field. . . . The old man wasn't chasing them—just the roof of his house showing above the trees, the dead elm . . . Tim skirted a clump of cedars. Dwayne was sitting in the weeds, tying his sneaker. He was still breathing hard. "Crud. If he'd had his gun right inside the door."

"You think he saw who we were?"

"Naw, he probably can't see ten feet. Crud. When he began yelling like that, I thought I'd piss my pants."

They set off cross-lots for home.

"He must have seen it was two of us though. Suppose he comes around asking?"

"My father'd kick his ass for him. He says you can smell him clear across the road when he goes by."

Mrs. Turner was in the kitchen. Tim took off his boots in the entryway and then went up to his room and sat down on the bed. . . . Dwayne had only broken that jar, mixed up the glop. Unless he'd done other stuff while Tim was waiting outside. If the police came, Mrs. Turner wouldn't know what they were talking about at first, she'd . . . Tim went into Larry and Peter's room and looked out the window at the empty road, the bridge. . . . The back door slammed. A man's voice he didn't recognize. He could hide till his mother got home, under the eaves in the closet in the playroom, Mrs. Turner calling and calling him. He tiptoed into his room and listened at the stairs.

"Well, if he wants more, tell him I'll have it next week. I'm going to cut up on Benedict's."

"What're they doing up there? I hear . . ."

Tim pressed his cheek against the window.

He could see the end of a truck loaded with wood in the driveway. Probably just Mr. Baker. A car stopped behind the truck. Tim drew back. His mother came toward the house, her arms loaded with packages. She stopped to talk to Mr. Baker. Tim sat down on his bed. He'd tried to stop Dwayne. He heard his mother come in downstairs.

"Are the boys home?"

"Tim's upstairs. The others said they was going up on the hill."

"Tim," his mother called. "Come down."

She didn't sound as if she knew. He went slowly downstairs.

"Yeah?"

"I bought you a candy bar. On the counter. And I finally found the right clock," she said to Mrs. Turner, taking a package out of one of the bags.

He watched her showing Mrs. Turner the new kitchen clock. What would she do if she found out? Make him sit in her study by himself till dinner? Then she'd come and talk to him. As if he'd burned down the house or something. If Larry and Peter did something, she just sent them to their room.

He went back upstairs. Someone had probably seen them on the road—the cars going by . . . He put the candy bar on his bed table. Maybe the old man wouldn't bother to try to find out who'd done it. They'd never hear anything more about it . . . as if it'd never happened.

At supper his mother asked him why he was so quiet. She felt his forehead.

"I've just got a little headache."

He tried to act interested. He'd decided if nobody came before dinner, he'd be safe. . . . But the old man shuffled along so slowly. . . . Mom telling about something that had happened while she was shopping, Dad carving roast beef for Peter—everything was like it had always been; nothing would happen. He'd never do it again. It'd been Dwayne's fault anyway . . .

"Tim? More roast beef?"

"No thank you."

He watched his father cutting off a piece of gristle for himself. The time Larry and Peter had broken his drill, he'd slammed the back door so hard the glass had cracked; a few minutes later Tim had heard Larry and Peter start to cry up in their room. . . . He ate the last mouthful of squash. If he'd just stayed home and played with his soldiers . . . Tomorrow he'd spend the whole day cleaning up his room, even drag all the boxes out from under the bed. . . .

"Tim, are you finished?" asked his mother.

He nodded, laying his fork on his plate.

"Can't we have ice cream?" Peter asked.

Tim wiped his mouth with his napkin and folded it carefully beside his plate. He wondered what Larry and Peter would say if they found out. They'd stolen a jar of buttons from the attic of Jimmy's old house last summer, but the bigger kids had been fooling around in there for months before that—the windows broken, an old couch rotting in the front yard. . . . Tim heard the back door open . . . Mrs. Turner calling the cats . . .

VII

After breakfast Tim dragged all the boxes out from under his bed and began to sort through them. . . . The back door slammed, the cats meowing—his mother'd probably given them the leftover cereal from breakfast. Larry and Peter went out—the *thump thump* of the basketball . . . Tim dumped out his cigar box of magic tricks on the rug. . . .

"Tim, I'm going to Cambridge." His mother stopped in the doorway. "Oh, *Tim.*"

"Mom, look, remember that trick I could never do?" He stood up among the litter of boxes and toys. "I'm going to clean it all up. I'm cleaning my room. But remember this trick I could never do?"

She watched him trying to palm the penny. "Do you want to come with me to Cambridge? Mrs. Turner will be here soon."

"Haber's? Yeah!" He stepped over some boxes and pulled open the drawer of his bed table. "I can get the Russian machine gunners."

"Hurry then. I'm leaving right away." She went on down the hall.

He began to count his money. . . . There was only two dollars and . . . He'd had eight dollars and something; he'd counted it last week. He pulled the drawer all the way out . . . *Dwayne*? They'd started playing Monopoly, then they'd had the argument and decided to go to the old man's . . .

"Tim? Are you coming?"

He'd gone to the playroom to get his boots. Dwayne had been left all alone.

"Tim?"

"No. No, I guess I won't go."

"I thought you wanted to buy something?" His mother put down the shopping bag she was carrying and started to rummage through her pocketbook.

"No." He felt as if he was going to cry . . . it was so stupid.

She glanced at him. The bank lay overturned on the bed.

"Did Dwayne steal your money?"

He picked up the bank. "I probably just lost it."

"Tim, look at me."

He shrugged, glancing up at her. It was stupid.

"Don't you want to come anyway?"

"No. I guess I better clean up."

"All right. We'll talk about it when I get back."

"Yeah, okay."

She went down the stairs. He began to dump stuff back into the boxes. Peter came in.

"He's stealing from *you* now, huh? Everybody told you he would. What'd you let him come in for?"

Tim stumbled over a box, starting downstairs. It didn't matter what they said. If everyone'd just leave him alone. They always said everything he did was wrong. . . . At the bottom of the stairs he glimpsed an old man coming onto the porch outside. *Him.* The door bell rang. Tim turned to go back up. Larry and Peter were coming down. His mother's footsteps; the door opening.

"You got a boy?"

"A boy?" His mother didn't understand. She sounded frightened. Larry and Peter leaned over him to see who it was.

"Two boys come into my house yestiddy. Threw my things all over, broke windows. You want me to get the sheriff?"

"I'm sure it couldn't have been . . ."

"Mrs. Bentley seen 'em comin' out of the woods, two of 'em, your boy and another. I ain't askin' much, jus' be paid for what they done."

Tim hadn't thought the old man would talk loud and demand things like an ordinary person. He was so old and dirty, bearded, shuffling. Tim had seen him once in Bentley's Store counting out change for something, mumbling to himself, not paying any attention to the people waiting behind him. Finally Mr. Bentley had taken the last twenty-five or thirty cents out of his hand, and the old man had turned and shuffled out without looking up, his head wagging.

"I ain't rich like some people . . . bottles and crud all over the floor. If I ain't paid, the sheriff'll hear about it. Kids nowadays think they can do what they want. Mrs. Bentley seen 'em comin' out of the woods. Windows broke, clothes all tore up."

"My husband's not home now. Could you . . ."

"I ain't askin' that much. Mrs. Bentley'll tell you, she seen 'em comin' out onto the road. I ain't got ever'thin' like some people . . . worked all my life . . ."

"How much . . . do you know how much it would come to?"

"Ketchup and syrup poured all over the floor, bedclothes tore up . . ."

"Twenty dollars? Would twenty dollars cover the damage?"

"I ain't found my hatchet yet, boxes pulled down all over the floor."

"You wait now. All right? I'll go get my pocketbook?"

"Mrs. Bentley seen 'em, two of 'em . . . bottles all broke . . ."

Tim heard the door shut, his mother go into the kitchen.

"Geez, it was you and Dwayne?" Larry and Peter looked around at him.

The cats were meowing and scratching at the screen around the old man. Tim squirmed past Larry and Peter and scrambled silently back up the stairs, tears starting in his eyes. She'd come up when the old man left. If he tried to hide, she'd find him.

"There. There's twenty dollars. And my husband will come and see you tonight to make sure . . ."

If he ran away, snuck out the front door . . .

"She's calling Dad," whispered Larry behind him. "Geez, you really wrecked the old man's house?"

"Were you stealing stuff?"

His bank was still lying open on the bed. What would they do to him? His father banging him down in a chair when he wouldn't stop teasing Larry, dragging and jerking him by the arm all the way back up the beach that time he'd spit . . . They could do anything to him, they could kill him even.

."Larry, you and Peter go downstairs." His mother came into the room. "Did you do it?"

He didn't answer. She knew he'd done it. What was she going . . .

"*Look at me!*" She pulled him around and held his shoulders. He didn't look up at her. She hadn't changed her sneakers to go to Cambridge yet. "*Look at me!*" She pushed up his chin. He jerked his head away. She held his chin up, hurting him. "Did you?"

"Yes."

"Look at me."

He looked up. He hated her, her hair pulled back in a bun, her face was so big, the wrinkles around her eyes, her red skin, she had hairs on her upper lip. "Did you?"

"Yes."

"How *could* you? An old man."

She'd been scared of him; her voice had trembled.

"Put on your pajamas and get into bed. Your father is coming." She slapped him. "Do you hear me?"

She let go of his shoulder and turned away to pull down the shade on his window. He fumbled with the buttons of his shirt, trying not to cry. She shut the door to Larry and Peter's room, picked up his Levi's. He got into his pajamas and into bed.

"Now if I hear you out of bed for any reason, any reason at all, you will be punished even more severely, do you understand?"

"Yes."

She went out. He lay under the covers in the strange half-light. It wasn't even time for lunch yet. He'd have to stay in bed all afternoon, then all night. Even the closed doors looked strange—blank, as if they'd never open again, or as if beyond them everything was changing—when he opened the door to go to the bathroom tomorrow morning, years and years would have passed outside, the ceilings tumbling in, grass growing up between the floorboards, birds flying in and out of the broken windows . . . like coming out of a movie into a hot, sunny afternoon. If he'd just come home when Dwayne wanted to go inside. Tiny specks of dust danced slowly in the streak of sunlight slanting past the edge of the shade onto the table. He lay still under the covers, waiting . . .

A car. Footsteps on the porch. The back door slammed. He heard his father's voice, then a door shutting. He wondered if the old man had gone to Dwayne's house, too. The door to Larry and Peter's room opened quietly.

"Boy, are they mad."

Tim raised himself on his elbow.

"Mom's crying because she was so scared, the old man acting so crazy."

"Did Dwayne *make* you do it?"

Tim lay back down, turning to the wall.

"Dad says his father gets drunk all the time."

"*Larry*," whispered Peter.

Their father was coming up the stairs. The door of their room clicked softly shut behind them.

"All right. Tell me what happened." His father sat down on the bed.

Tim began to cry.

"Come on. Tell me what happened."

"I just wanted to see what it was like inside and then Dwayne started doing things."

"What? Tell me."

Tim told him everything he could remember. "But after I came out because I was scared, he was still doing stuff, I could hear him."

"Did either of you take anything?"

"I didn't see him. *I* didn't."

"It was the same boy who stole things from Larry and Peter and your mother?"

Tim nodded, wondering what his father would do, the tears drying on his cheeks.

"All right." His father stood up. "Now look, it's no excuse to say the other boy did everything, and you just watched. You should have stopped him or come away and told somebody. But I guess you're not old enough yet to stand up for what your mother and I have tried to teach you." His father picked up a soldier and set it on the bed table. "Now your mother and I can't watch you every minute, so I'm not going to tell you to stay away from the boy. You'll have to decide that for yourself. You know what we think about it—one of these days he's going to get himself into some really serious trouble. But I don't want him in the house, I don't want to see him hanging around here. Do you understand?"

Tim nodded.

"You know . . . Look, I know Larry and Peter are sort of rough on you sometimes. But they aren't going to get you into anything like tearing up some old man's house."

"Yeah. And they don't steal stuff from me."

"Right. Now you stay in your room today. I want you to think about what you did. Think what it. would be like to come back from school some day and find this room all torn apart, your things stepped on and broken, your bottle of glue there dripped all over everything.

"You stay *in* bed with the shade *down*. And tomorrow you can start earning back the twenty dollars your mother gave the old man, cleaning up around the woodpile and along the back fence. And no television for two weeks. I want you to understand how serious this was. It wasn't just mischief. You were destroying somebody else's property, and you were doing it because you didn't think he mattered, he was old and a little crazy and so he didn't matter. But everybody matters, not just what you want or what I want. Okay? Now I'm going back to work, and your mother's taking Larry and Peter to Cambridge, but Mrs. Turner is here. I've told her you're to stay in your room."

"Does she know what happened?"

"We're not going to try to hide something like this, Tim. You should know what other people think about it."

Tim heard the door of his mother's study shut, then after a long while his father saying something to Mrs. Turner in the entryway. The back door slammed. His mother called Larry and Peter; the vacuum cleaner started up in the dining room. He turned over so that he was facing the wall; if Mrs. Turner looked in, she'd think he was sleeping. A crack ran up the wallpaper like a road, the flowers were parks, he'd made that gouge trying to hammer in a nail—he couldn't remember why . . . Dwayne ladling the glop into the dishes . . . he'd told him to stop. But not because of the mess—he'd just been scared they'd get caught, the old man would come back while they were inside the house . . . Except they would have heard him on the porch or going around through the weeds. Maybe Dwayne just didn't

care about anything, he didn't care *what* he
did. All afternoon, all the time they were in the
old man's house, coming home, he'd had the
money he'd stolen in his pocket. Tim reached
up and scraped at the plaster under the
gouged wallpaper with his fingernail. Maybe
Dwayne never worried about anything, never
got scared. Except he'd acted sort of scared of
his father. When his father'd sworn at him,
he'd just stood there. Tim wondered if he
should ask Mrs. Turner for a glass of milk.
He could get his flashlight and read comic
books under the covers . . .

VIII

"Tim?"

His mother was standing over him with a tray. She rested a corner of the tray on the bed table and turned on the lamp. He sat up.

"Hungry?"

"Yeah." He nodded.

"Lean forward." She plumped his pillows up behind him and then set the tray on his legs. He began to eat. She straightened the blankets at the end of the bed and then sat down on them.

"Have you thought about what Daddy said?"

He nodded.

She watched him eating his hamburger. "It's so important to try to think what other people are feeling. I suppose it was fun to mix the ketchup and sugar and things into a soup . . ."

"I didn't. Dwayne did it."

"Well, then it was fun to watch. But if you and Dwayne had thought about how the old man would feel when he came home and saw the mess, perhaps you wouldn't have done it."

"Yeah." Except Dwayne probably wouldn't have cared. "Do you think he steals stuff just because he's poor?"

"No. Jimmy Skidmore never took anything."

Tim began to eat his peas. His mother slid the shade up. Outside it was almost dark, the trees black against the luminous sky.

"I don't really know why Dwayne does it. Maybe his parents never taught him he shouldn't. Maybe he just wants something so badly he can't stop himself, even though he knows it's wrong. . . . Would you like some more milk?"

"No. No thank you."

"How much did Dwayne take from your bank?"

"Six dollars and ninety cents. Are you going to make him give back what he stole?"

"I think he'd just say he didn't take it."

"I'm really not going to play with him anymore, even other places. He gets into too much trouble."

"I don't think he's the kind of boy you can be friends with now. Perhaps when he gets older, he'll be able to see things differently. Right now he seems to be a very troubled little boy." She brushed back his hair and then picked up the tray. "I'll be back to tuck you in."

"Do I get any dessert?"

"Not tonight. Daddy and I want you to really think about what you did."

Larry and Peter had gone out somewhere after breakfast. His mother was typing in her study. Tim slid the airplane gingerly into the hangar of blocks and stood up. . . . Someone was coming across the driveway. Dwayne. He ducked down. A knock on the back door.

"Is Tim around?"

"Yes."

"Can he come out?"

"I'm afraid he won't be able to come out for a long time after what happened the other day, Dwayne. His father and I think it would be better if he played by himself or with his brothers for a while."

Tim heard the door shut, his mother go back through the dining room. Maybe the old man hadn't gone to Dwayne's house, so he'd figured Tim's mother and father wouldn't know, either. Tim went quietly into Larry and Peter's room, to the front window. Dwayne was going off down the road toward the bridge . . . Nobody'd tried to get him to stop stealing. Tim's mother could have talked to him or gone to see his mother. All the stuff about what the old man had felt like. But nobody had bothered about how Dwayne would feel when he was told he couldn't come around anymore. Last night when Peter had been in Bentley's Store with Dad, Mr. Bentley'd said the old man had probably just wanted the money to get drunk on.

Dwayne had stopped on the bridge, looking down at the water. Tim wondered what would have happened if he'd told him that Larry and Peter knew he was taking stuff. Dwayne would probably just have beaten him up. He was like Larry and Peter, he only wanted to do what *he* wanted.

Dwayne disappeared around the bushes on the other side of the bridge . . .

Tim took the muskrat claw out of his pocket and smelled it; he'd put salt on it. He could set out his own traps . . . Larry and Peter'd never set out traps; they didn't even know you were supposed to chain a trap to something. . . .

MS READ-a-thon —
a simple way to start
youngsters reading

Boys and girls between 6 and 14 can join the MS READ-a-thon and help find a cure for Multiple Sclerosis by reading books. And they get two rewards — the enjoyment of reading, and the great feeling that comes from helping others.

Parents and educators: For complete information call your local MS chapter. Or mail the coupon below.

Kids can help, too!